The Thief

Ruth Rendell

arrow books

Published by Arrow in 2006

1 3 5 7 9 10 8 6 4 2

CHAPTER ONE

THE FIRST TIME SHE stole something Polly was eight years old. She and her mother had gone in the car to have tea with her aunt, so that she could play with her cousins, James and Lizzie. It was a fine sunny day in the middle of summer. Chairs and tables were out in the garden under a big sunshade. There was a blow-up pool and the hose was on. James and Lizzie were in swimsuits and Polly put hers on. They splashed about in the water. Polly got very excited, splashed water over her mother and Auntie Pauline and took hold of Lizzie, holding her head under the water. Her mother told her to stop and then, when Polly didn't stop, she told her again.

'Stop that at once, Polly. You're spoiling the game for the others!'

Polly had stopped for a while, then begun again, splashing with both hands. Her aunt got up, said to her, 'Come into the house. I've got something I want to show you.'

So Polly got out of the water, dried herself on a towel and followed Auntie Pauline into the house. She thought she was going to get a present. Auntie Pauline had said that once before and had given her the thing she had shown her. Not this time. As soon as they were inside and the door was shut her aunt put her over her knee and smacked her hard, ten sharp blows across her bottom. Then Auntie Pauline went back into the garden.

When her aunt had gone and left her crying, Polly had hated her. She would have liked to kill her. Rubbing her eyes, she had walked slowly through the rooms. In one of them was a desk and on the desk, lying face-down, the book Auntie Pauline was reading. Polly took it. She put it in the big bag her mother had left in the hallway. It wasn't her aunt's book but one from the Public Library. If it was missing Auntie Pauline would have to pay for it . . .

When it was time to go, she and her mother got into the car and while her mother was driving Polly took the book out of her bag and hid it under her jacket. She meant to destroy it.

But how? There was nowhere to burn it. She found her mother's scissors and while her parents were watching the news on TV she went up to her bedroom and cut the book into a hundred small pieces.

Polly's mother and Auntie Pauline had a lot of talks about the missing book. Polly was always there and heard what they said. Where could the book have gone? Auntie Pauline had asked everyone, Uncle Martin and Lizzie and James and the lady who came to clean. No one knew anything about it.

'You haven't seen it, have you, Polly?' her mother asked.

Polly looked her right in the eyes. 'Oh, no, Mummy, of course I haven't.'

She was a good liar. It seemed too that she was a good thief.

In the same class at school there was a girl called Abigail Robinson. She wasn't one of Polly's crowd. Polly thought Abby was the only person in the class who didn't like her. No, it wasn't a matter of not liking. Abby really disliked her. And it was more than that; not hating but despising. Abby looked at her as if she was

3

something dirty you trod in in the street. And she never spoke to Polly if she could help it.

One day Polly said to her, 'What's wrong with me, I'd like to know?'

Abby just shrugged her shoulders.

'My mother says you've got an attitude problem,' Polly said.

Her mother hadn't said this. She knew nothing about Abby Robinson and her not speaking to Polly.

'I suppose that's a lie,' said Abby. '*Another* lie. You're always lying. That's why I don't want to know you.'

Abby had a watch she was very proud of. It was gold with a dark green face and gold hands. At swimming class she left it on a shelf in the changing room and when everyone else had gone into the pool Polly hung back and took Abby's watch. She put it in the pocket of her school blazer and put the blazer in her locker.

After the class Abby couldn't find her watch and there was a hunt for it. Polly didn't stay to join the hunt. It was three-thirty, time to go home. When she got home she went into the shed where her father kept his tools and smashed the watch with a hammer. Then, carrying the pieces, she went out into the street and dropped the remains of the watch down the drain.

Everyone at school was asked about the missing watch. The head teacher asked Polly along with the rest of her class. She looked into the head teacher's eyes, stared into her eyes, and put on her honest face.

'I never saw it, Mrs Wilson,' she said. 'I haven't touched it.'

And all the time she had a little cut on her hand where a piece of broken glass had scratched her.

Stealing things from people who had upset her was something Polly did quite a lot. Only she didn't call it stealing but 'taking'. Later on, when she was older, she had a boyfriend called Tom. He was a student and he hadn't much money. Music was what he loved and he loved his CD Walkman too. Polly thought he loved it much more than he loved her. She was right, he did, and after they had been together for a year he told her he wanted them to split up.

'I can't take you lying all the time,' he said. 'I never know what the truth is any more with you. You even lie about the time you left work or where you've been if you're late or who you've met. It's just easier for you to lie so you do it.'

'I don't,' she said. 'I don't. Tell me just one lie I've told.'

'You said the phone didn't ring while I was out but I know it did. It must have rung three times. That's one. You said you didn't have a drink with Alex Swain last night but I know you did. John saw you. They say that even a liar must tell more truths than lies but you tell more lies than truths.'

He said he'd be moving out the next day. She took his Walkman while he was in the shower. He had left it lying in the bedroom on a chair on top of his jacket, a round blue and silver Walkman. She picked it up, ran down the stairs with it and out into the street. The place they lived in was at a crossroads with traffic lights. It was early morning and the traffic was heavy with big lorries waiting at the red light before taking the M1 up to the north. Polly was excited and breathing heavily. When the traffic light turned green, she threw the Walkman into the road, in front of a big truck. She heard the crunching cracking sound when the huge wheels went over it.

Tom knew he had left it somewhere in the room and he hunted everywhere for it. Of course he asked Polly if she had seen it. She looked him in the eye and told him she hadn't.

'I don't believe you.'

'Believe what you like,' she said. 'I haven't seen your stupid old Walkman. You must have left it somewhere.'

What could he do about it? He walked out on her the next day but not before he told her he had seen the broken blue and silver pieces in the road.

Polly wasn't alone for long. She started seeing Alex Swain and she fell in love with him. He fell in love with her too and they moved in together. Alex was different from any boyfriend she had had before. He was five years older with a house of his own and a car and a good job. Apart from that, he was a grown-up person who made rules for life and kept them. As well as being very good-looking, Alex was kind and loving and, above all, an honest man who valued truth-telling. He often said how much he hated lying, even the kind of lies people tell

7

to get out of going somewhere they don't want to go. Even the lies they tell to avoid hurting someone's feelings. If you spoke firmly and with kindness, he said, you need not lie.

Being with him changed Polly's life. Or she thought it had changed her life. She found that Alex trusted her. He took it for granted what she said to him was the truth. He believed everything she said. And because she loved him she mostly told him the truth. It wasn't hard to be truthful with him.

He is making me a better person, she said to herself. I am young enough to change. It's lucky for me I met him while I was still young. Another thing he did for her was that he taught her not to hate people. It wasn't worth it, he said. And now she was with him no one seemed to hurt or upset her or if they did she had learned to forget it. She no longer took other people's things and broke them. If they were unkind to her or let her down in some way, she didn't hate them as she once would have done. All that was in the past. She was different.

'I've never known you so happy, Polly,' her mother said. 'Being with Alex must be doing you good.'

8

And her friend Louise said, 'I thought he was a bit too much of a do-gooder but I've changed my mind now I see he's making you happy.'

CHAPTER TWO

ALEX SAW THE SUITCASE before Polly did. It was quite a small suitcase, orange with a black trim and a black and orange strap, surely the only one like it in the airport.

'He won't lose it,' he said. 'No one will pick that up by mistake.'

Polly laughed. 'I'd get tired of it if it was mine.'

The man with the suitcase wore a black suit and a bright yellow shirt. He was ahead of them in the queue at the check-in and there were three people between them and him. The queue moved very slowly.

'You may as well go,' said Polly. 'There's no point in you waiting. I'll be back on Friday.'

'I just thought I'd like to see you safely through the fast-track but if you're really sure. I do have things to do.'

Alex kissed her and she watched him go back

the way they had come. He looked back twice, waving. The man in black and yellow had reached the check-in desk and put his orange case on the conveyor. His name in large black letters on an orange label was easy to read: *Trevor Lant*. One thing to be said for a bag that colour, thought Polly, was that you'd see it the moment it bowled out on to the belt. There wouldn't be any puzzling over which of the black ones was yours. The man in the black suit had been given his boarding pass and was off towards the gate with his small but still orange carry-on bag. Moving up the queue, Polly forgot him.

Forgot him, that is, until he was at the gate. She saw him again then, could hardly have missed him, for Trevor Lant had taken over four of the chairs in the seating area. It looked as if the flight would be full and all those waiting wanted to sit down. Lant had spread his things out to cover those chairs, the small orange carry-on bag, two newspapers, a magazine, his suit jacket, a book and a slice of cake in plastic wrap. Polly moved into the seating area just as a woman went up to Lant and asked him if he would mind moving his

11

things so that she and her mother could sit down.

'Yes, I would mind.' Lant stared at her. 'First come, first served. You should have got here sooner if you wanted a seat.'

The woman blushed. She had lost her nerve and walked away. An old man tried it next, then a woman with a shrill voice.

'What's with you people?' said Lant. 'Didn't you hear me the first time? I'm not moving my stuff.'

'I'm afraid you'll have to, sir.' This was one of the women from behind the desk, fetched from looking at boarding passes. 'There's a lady here who can't stand for long. Now come along, I'm sure you don't want any trouble.'

'Yes, I do,' Lant said. 'I don't mind a bit of trouble. It would liven things up a bit, would trouble. I'm getting bored out of my head in this dump. Go on, move my stuff, and you'll see what trouble is.'

Polly didn't wait to hear the outcome. She moved away and stood staring out of one of the windows at the Boeing 757 which in half an hour would start taking them all to New York. Behind him voices were raised, a crowd had gathered and men in uniform had joined in. But just as she began to think that the man in the black suit would not be allowed to stay in the seating area, the flight was called and boarding began. Trevor Lant slowly picked up his newspapers, his book, his jacket, his piece of cake and his orange carry-on bag and joined the queue.

With a club class ticket, Polly thought herself safe from him. She was almost sure she had seen an economy class ticket in his hand. But a passenger may be upgraded to a higher class and it seemed this had been done for Lant. He had been given the seat beside Polly's and would be sitting next to her for the next seven hours.

At first this seemed no problem. Lant said not a word. He gave his jacket to a member of the crew, stuffed his book and papers into the pocket in front of him and put his orange bag on the floor. His seatbelt on, he lay back and closed his eyes. He looked about thirty-five. He had dark hair, very pale skin and thin lips. She remembered that his teeth were good, his eyes blue. Most people would call him attractive but he was so very rude. I hope he won't be rude to me, she thought. I hate that.

13

Polly turned her head to the window, thinking that she had never known a flight to take off on time. This one left only ten minutes late. She had a book with her and the crossword puzzle in the paper to do. A trolley came round and she took a glass of wine, then another. Alex didn't like her to drink too much but Alex wasn't here. She read the paper. There was a story about an escaped Komodo dragon with a photo. It was the stuff of nightmares, a giant lizard.

Lant slept on. Polly was handed a menu and one for the man next to her. Lunch came quickly after that and the rattle of her table woke Lant. He sat up with a jerk, nearly hitting the tray the stewardess was passing her.

'You might have told me lunch was coming,' he said to Polly in a sharp tone. 'You should have woken me up.'

The stewardess caught her eye and gave a little smile. It was plain she thought Polly and Lant were partners. That was how it sounded. Polly didn't return the look or reply to Lant. He said to her, 'I'm Trevor. What's your name?'

'Polly,' she said.

He made a big fuss over putting up his table,

14

tugging at it and pushing it too far forward. She had pasta for her main course and he had chicken curry. Polly was hungry and had eaten most of hers when Lant set down his knife and fork and said, 'How's your food, Polly? Vile, isn't it?'

This time she had to say something, though she was smarting from being treated like a doormat kind of wife. 'Mine wasn't bad.'

'You tell them that and the standard will never get better. It will just go down. I don't know what's with you people. You put up with second-class everything. Have you no taste? Don't you care?'

Before she could reply, he was saying the same thing to the stewardess who came to take their plates. She was to tell the cook, if there was a cook, repeat his very words and come back and tell him she had done so. The stewardess said she would and Polly asked her if she would bring her another glass of wine. What Lant said next took her breath away.

'It's not a good idea drinking alcohol on flights. These glasses are very big. Each one is at least four units and you're quite a small woman.'

She wanted to say she needed it, having to sit next to him but she never said things like that. She wasn't very brave. If she was rude to him she was afraid he would insult her, make some remark about her looks or her clothes and that would hurt. He was looking over her shoulder at the photo of the giant lizard.

'I was talking to you,' he said.

'I know,' she said.

'Here's your poison coming now. Make it last. You don't want to stagger off the plane when we get there.'

The stewardess began to tell him that the chief steward had apologised. They were sorry the food hadn't been to his liking. Would he accept a glass of dessert wine?

'I don't drink,' he said. 'Give it to her. She can put any amount away.'

That was too much for Polly. She told herself, you will regret it if you don't speak up now, and said, 'Are you always so rude? I don't want to talk to you. Why can't you leave me alone?'

Her hands were shaking and he could see. He laughed. 'Poor little Polly. Was Daddy horrid then?'

16

She felt her face grow red. It was always the way. She could never match someone else's rudeness. Her hands would shake, she would blush and come out with words a child might use. She had other ways of dealing with it but these were not possible now. His next words surprised her.

'You know what they say. If a man's rude to a woman it's because he finds her attractive.'

'Do they?' She had never heard anyone say it.

'You are, though. Very attractive. Have dinner with me tonight?'

She wouldn't dream of it. Have him call her a poor little thing and tell her to stop drinking? Well, she could try to be rude, even if she blushed and her hands shook.

'I'd rather have dinner with the Komodo dragon,' she said very loudly.

Now she had got to him. His face went red and white and set in rigid lines. She turned away with a toss of her head and looked out of the window, seeing nothing. A voice saying 'Would you like coffee?' made her turn round. She nodded, and passed the cup from her tray. He had coffee too. They sat, staring in front of them, each with a cup of coffee.

Because she was going straight to a meeting with friends as soon as they got to New York, she was wearing a pale cream trouser suit. The airline's paper napkin was across her knees. She put milk into her coffee, stirred it. His voice saying 'Watch this' turned her head. He lifted his cup and poured a stream of coffee across her knee.

It was hot and Polly screamed. The stewardess came running.

'He poured coffee over me,' she cried. 'He poured it over me on purpose. He's mad.'

The stewardess looked from one to the other. 'I'm sure he didn't mean . . .'

'Of course I didn't,' Lant said. 'Of course not. I'm so sorry, Polly. I can't tell you how sorry I am. What can I do? Can I pay your cleaning bill?'

She said nothing. She was afraid that if she spoke she would start to cry. The stewardess sponged her trousers but the stain wouldn't come out. Polly thought of how she would have to meet her friends with a big brown stain from the top of her thigh to her knee. She would have no time to change. Could they give her a different seat? The chief steward said he was sorry but there were no empty seats.

She went back to sit next to Lant. Her leg smarted where the hot coffee had touched the skin. She put the airline's blanket over her knees to cover the stain. Tears were running out of her eyes. She closed them and turned her face into the back of the seat. He was sleeping, breathing heavily, and his breathing sounded to her like laughter.

You are not a child, she told herself. Stop crying, don't let him see. I hate him, a voice inside her said, I hate him. I would like to kill him. She thought of other people she had hated like this, her Auntie Pauline, a girl at school, a boyfriend who had left her. She had had revenge on them. Revenge wasn't possible with Trevor Lant. Her tears dry now, she sat there for hours, quieter, telling herself, you will never see him again after we land. Never again.

She dozed. The captain's voice, saying they were beginning their descent for New York, woke her. Lant was still asleep.

19

CHAPTER THREE

WITH TEN MINUTES TO spare before her friends
were due, Polly changed her trousers for a black
pair in the hotel bathroom. Next morning she
tried three dry-cleaners but they all said the
stain would never come out, though one said
they would try. She had come to New York to
go to her cousin Lizzie's wedding and she
meant to have a happy day. Before leaving for
the church she spoke on the phone to Alex. She
had thought to tell him about Trevor Lant and
what he had said. But somehow, when she was
talking to him, she couldn't. If she started that
she would have to tell him what she had said to
Lant when he asked her to have dinner with
him. He would be shocked. He hated rudeness.

'Did you have a good flight?'

'Oh, yes. Quite good.'

'No one awful sitting next to you?'

Now would be the time to tell him. Instead,

she lied. He was so kind and trusting he always believed her.

'No. The seat was empty all the way to New York.'

'I hope you'll be as lucky coming back. I miss you, darling.'

'I miss you too.'

Why had she lied to Alex? An ex-boyfriend had told her she lied when there was no need. She could have told Alex a man had sat next to her and nothing more than that. But she had lied. And it was the first time for weeks.

She went to the wedding. Her Auntie Pauline was there as the bride's mother and she greeted Polly at the church door. Polly hadn't seen her very much for years. Auntie Pauline had changed a lot and looked quite old but she was still the same woman who had smacked Polly after saying she had something to show her. As Polly walked in and took her seat she thought again about taking the book and cutting it up. She looked at the little scar on her hand where a piece of glass had cut it. When the service started she forgot Auntie Pauline and the smacking and the book for a while and asked herself how she would feel if she was the bride and Alex the bridegroom. One day, she thought, maybe one fine day we'll get married.

Next day she was taken to the theatre. Then there was shopping and lunch with the friends she had met when she first got there. She didn't see Auntie Pauline again and someone told her she had gone back on Thursday morning. It was Thursday night when Polly took a taxi to the airport. She ought to buy a present to take home for Alex but he never seemed to want anything and in the end, after looking in shop windows, she left it.

Lant's case came into view before he did. She thought, it can't be, I'm seeing things. But there it was, in the economy class queue, and there he was in his black suit, a pink shirt this time and with his orange carry-on bag. She shouldn't have said what she had said to him. He wouldn't forget it. He was the kind of man who would want revenge and she knew all about revenge.

They wouldn't up him to club class this time. Surely they wouldn't. The queue he was in moved more slowly than hers. It was far longer. When she had checked in, she turned round and met his eyes. He curled his lip and made a gesture with the middle finger of his right hand.

22

She felt the blood rush into her face. Please let me get to the check-in fast and get away from him. When she was given her boarding pass, she sighed with relief and walked away as fast as she could.

The gate was a long way away but she would get there first. And then – would he come and sit next to her? It would be better if she didn't get there first. Let him get there first and then she could sit far away from him. You will soon be home, she told herself, and then you really will never see him again. He can't hurt you. Anyway, he will be sitting in the economy class. She went into a little bar, meaning to have a cup of coffee. When she was sitting on the bar stool she asked for a gin and tonic instead. She needed it.

If he passed by she didn't see him. But she couldn't sit there much longer. She had to go. In ten minutes the gate would close and in twenty boarding would begin. On her way to the gate she felt that at any moment he might come up behind her. Even touch her. It was like walking in a dark street at night and knowing someone was behind you. The footfalls come nearer but you mustn't run.

23

She looked round. The footfalls were a woman's. He was nowhere. He must be at the gate, she thought, and he was. He must have got there while she was having her drink but she hadn't seen him. She knew he must be there but still she jumped when she saw him. She sat down as far from him as she could get. Boarding began and when she joined the line he came up to her. Turning away, she pretended not to see him but he spoke to her. There was no escape.

'Remember me?' he said.

She nodded, her mouth dry.

'I think you should say you're sorry for what you said to me.'

She found a voice, a little shrill voice. 'I will not! That dragon is lovely beside you. Now go away.'

He shouted at her. 'You bitch! You stuck-up bitch!'

One of the airport staff came up to them. 'Now, sir, please. This won't do. Please keep your voice down.'

'Tell her,' Lant said. 'She's my partner. She flies club and makes me fly economy. How about that?'

Polly felt the tears come into her eyes. Her

'I'm not, I didn't,' sounded feeble. 'Let's just get on the aircraft,' she said, a sob in her voice.

And when they did, she was sent to the left and Lant to the right. He was quiet and meek now. He had got what he wanted and made the flight crew think she was his partner. She could see that in the looks they gave her. The stewardess thought she and Lant were a couple but she had made herself the boss and she had the money. What sort of woman would make her husband or lover or boyfriend travel economy while she went club? No wonder they all looked at her like that.

Still he had gone and had no reason to come down here. Early in the morning she would be in London and she would never see him again. Alex would be there to meet her. If only he were with her now! She longed to see him. If he were with her now, to hold her hand, to comfort her, to speak to Lant in the way only he could, calmly, quietly but very sternly. She did up her seatbelt, closed her eyes, pretended Lant wasn't there.

The flight took off. The aircraft came through the cloud cover into a clear blue sky. Polly had a pre-dinner drink and a small bottle of wine with her dinner. It would help her to sleep. Just before they put out the cabin lights, the stewardess came up to her and handed her a piece of paper.

'Your partner asked me to give you this.'

Polly fancied her tone was cold.

'Thank you.'

Why was the woman standing there?

'Can I get you anything before we dim the lights?'

'No, thank you. I'm fine.'

The piece of paper was folded once. She was sure the stewardess had read it. Of course she had. Polly opened it. *Don't binge-drink,* it said. *You are an alcoholic and I am keeping my eye on you.*

She would have liked to kill him. If he were beside her now she would hit him. She couldn't help herself. Often she slept on flights but now she couldn't. She kept thinking of the stewardess reading that note, telling the rest of the crew. Maybe Trevor Lant talked to them about her and asked them to keep an eye on her. Maybe he talked to the people next to him, pointed her out, said she was a worry to him. Hit him, go down there and hit him, if only she dared. She lay awake all night, turning from side to side, thinking of Auntie Pauline hitting her in the garden. And what she had done. Long ago, twenty years ago, but still fresh in her mind.

Another note came in the morning. This time she didn't look at it. She knew it would be about her drinking. She meant to stop anyway, not because of Lant but because Alex didn't like it. Now she told herself that the club class would get off first. When they landed she would be among the first ten or twelve to get off. He would be far behind.

Getting up and moving to the exit, she took care not to look to her left. She kept her eyes fixed ahead. She was the fifth person to step off the aircraft and she walked fast. Along the passages, following the signs, keeping in fifth place, joining the EU line, showing her passport and passing through. Then and only then she looked back. Lant was nowhere to be seen.

Down the ramp to the baggage hall. Take a trolley. The bags from the New York flight started coming through soon after she got there. For the first time ever her case was one of the first to roll down the belt. She took hold of it and put it on the trolley. As she began to wheel it away she saw the orange one bounce on to the belt. Lant's orange suitcase with the black trim.

Hatred for him filled her and made her heart pound. She turned round and went back, watching the orange case go round. There was a pale blue one in front of it and a black one behind. Most of the baggage was black. His was the only orange one. She stood there, waiting – for what? For him to come? The bags were coming round again. A grey one first, then a dark red one with a strap round it, then the pale blue one. Without thinking what she was doing, Polly put out her arm, grabbed the orange case by its handle and pulled it off the belt. She put it next to hers on the trolley and wheeled it away. Her heart beat heavily. She was tense with fear and joy. She had done it, she had got back at him. This was her revenge. As soon as she could she would destroy his case.

It was only when she was through Customs that she thought how the orange case would be known everywhere. No one else had one like it. Alex would know it as soon as he saw it. She went into the ladies' toilet, leaving the trolley outside. With her case and Lant's inside a cubicle, the door locked, she opened the orange case. No time to see what was in it. She pulled everything out, most of it in plastic bags but dirty clothes as well. On the outward trip her own case had been half-full of presents for Lizzie and other friends. With the presents gone, there was plenty of room. She stuffed Lant's things in and shut the lid.

The orange case must stay behind. She found a piece of paper in her handbag, and wrote on it *Out of Order*. She unlocked the door, said to the woman waiting, 'Don't go in there. It's dirty. It's a mess', and fixed the notice on the door handle. Hours would pass before they found the orange case.

All his stuff would be rubbish, she thought. Everything he had with him would be rubbish – but not to him. The loss of it would spoil his day and next day and the next. It would cost him a lot of money. It would cause him endless trouble. Good. She would destroy it all. Of course she would. She always destroyed the stuff she took.

It was a long time since she had taken anything. Years. She remembered taking Tom's

Walkman. To get back at him. To have revenge because he told her she was a liar and he couldn't stand her lying. But this must be the last. Never do it again, she told herself. You are going to be like Alex, honest, truthful, a fit wife for him . . .

Lant would be in the baggage hall by now. He would be watching all the other cases coming off, all but his. He would go to that lost baggage counter you went to and tell them. It would be a long time before he guessed she had taken it – if he ever did.

Why did I do it? she asked herself as she came out into the cold London air. *Why do I do it?* Then Alex was there, kissing her, taking her own case from her. She walked beside him to the car.

'You're very silent,' he said. 'Are you all right?'

'I'm fine.'

Coming home was better than going away. Polly had felt like this only since she met Alex. Before that, home was just somewhere you slept and maybe ate your breakfast. This house was Alex's. He had bought it before she knew him and furnished it with things he had chosen carefully in colours he liked. When he first brought her here she had walked round, admiring everything. The people she knew didn't live in houses like this. It was a grown-up's house, full of pretty things Alex had looked after, china and glass and books, pictures and green plants, cushions and rugs. Polly knew Alex would have put flowers in the vases to welcome her home. Tulips and daffodils were in the hall, the first thing she saw when he opened the front door.

He had to leave for work almost at once. She wanted him to go so that she could open her case. Wanting Alex to go was new. She had never felt like that before but now she was longing to open her case. Alex took it upstairs into their bedroom and put it on the bed. He kissed her good-bye and said he'd be home by six. From the window she watched him get back into the car and reverse it out of the driveway.

All the way home she had looked forward to opening it. But now it was there and she was alone a strange thing happened. Opening it no longer seemed a good idea. She went up to it and put her hands on its lid. The scar on her left hand showed up more than usual. It looked red against her pale skin. Her hands rested there for a moment and then she took them away. She told herself that she wasn't exactly afraid of what she might see. It was just that there was no need to know now, at once, at this minute, what was in those plastic bags she had taken out of the orange case. Later would do. Put it off till later.

She took the case off the bed and laid it on the seat of a chair. Then she lay down on the bed, on top of the quilt. The sunshine was very bright. Should she draw the curtains? She got up and drew them. The curtains were the colour of a cornflower and now the room was full of a blue glow. She got back on the bed and turned to face the other way. In front of her eyes was the chair and on the seat was the case. Closing her eyes, she tried to sleep but the room was too light. It was hard to keep her eyes shut but when she opened them all she saw was the case. She got up again and put it on the floor where she couldn't see it.

The triumph she had felt when she first took the orange case was gone now. Already she was wishing she hadn't taken it. Tired as she was, she knew it was no use lying there. She wouldn't sleep. After a few more minutes of lying there in the soft blue light, she got up, drew back the curtains and went downstairs. She made herself a sandwich but she couldn't eat it. What she needed was a drink to help her open that case.

She poured gin into a glass, put in an ice cube and orange juice. That made her think of how Lant had called her an alcoholic. She felt better about taking his case. He had asked for it. He had asked for what she had done, talking to her like that. The gin was a good idea. Drinking it made her think she'd be able to open the case quite soon, though she still couldn't eat her sandwich. I had my revenge, she said to herself, going upstairs again, I had my revenge. I got back at him. She didn't feel excited and happy the way she had when she took Auntie Pauline's book. When she cut up the pages with her mother's scissors. Or when she took Abby Robinson's watch, smashed it with her father's hammer, pushed the bits down the drain and made that scar.

Maybe she didn't feel happy because she

hadn't yet destroyed what had been in his case. Breaking or burning or cutting up the things she took always seemed to take a load off her mind. That was how she got to feel better. Those plastic bags would hold only dirty clothes and maybe things he had bought. Cheap things, not worth much, but burning them or stamping on them and putting them in the rubbish would help her. She lifted up the case and put it back on the bed.

I have to get my own clothes out, she said to herself. I have to take his things out. Don't put it off any longer. Time is passing. It's already nearly three and Alex will be home again at six. But she did put it off. It was so long since she had taken anything of someone else's, destroyed anything. Because I didn't need to, she thought. Because I met Alex and I was happy. Was that it? I didn't tell so many lies too because I was happy. She walked to the window and looked down into the street below. Someone parked a red car on the other side. A woman came along with a small brown dog on a lead. Go back, she said to herself. Go back and open that case.

Suppose there was something dreadful inside.

But what could there be? Body parts, she thought, drugs. But no, those things would have been found. Porn? Well, if that was what it was, she would burn it. The best thing would be to burn everything. But where could she burn it? No one had open fires any more except maybe in the country. There was a metal bucket outside in the shed. She could make a fire in that. But she had never in all her life made a fire. It was something people used to do, when her mother was young.

Count to ten, she said aloud, and when you get to ten open the case. She counted to ten but she didn't open it. This was mad, this was no way to go on. She put her hands on the lid of the case and saw the scar again. She shut her eyes so that she couldn't see it, held her breath, and flung the lid open.

Lant's plastic bags lay jumbled up inside. She couldn't see what was inside them. Slowly, she took them out, laid them on the bed, feeling paper inside. She knew what was in them before she looked and she began to feel sick. One after another she opened the packets. Nothing dirty, nothing horrible. The packets were full of money, fifty-pound notes in one, US dollars in the next, euros in the third, hundreds if not thousands.

She ran into the bathroom and threw up into the basin.

CHAPTER FOUR

MONEY WAS THE ONE thing she couldn't destroy.
No matter how much she might want to. She
couldn't. Things, yes. A book, a watch, a
Walkman. That hadn't felt like stealing but like
revenge, like a trick, like getting her own back.
A man her father knew had been caught
stealing money from the firm he worked for.
Her mother and father had been shocked,
upset, and so had she when they told her. Now
she was as bad as that man, she had stolen
money. She could go to prison or, because it
was a first offence, get a fine and a criminal
record for the rest of her life.

Telling herself that she must know, there
must be no more putting off, she counted the
money. Five thousand pounds, a bit less than
ten thousand dollars, a bit under ten thousand
euros. Yet he had flown economy class. Because
he got the money in New York and he already

had his return ticket? Perhaps. What did it matter? The big thing, the awful thing, was that she had stolen it.

She couldn't leave it there on the bed. Time was passing and it was nearly four. At this time of year the sun had set, the light was going. She couldn't leave Lant's dirty clothes there either. Those she stuffed into one of the plastic bags, took it downstairs and put it outside into the wastebin. The afternoon felt cold now it was getting dark. A sharp wind was blowing.

Back in the bedroom, she counted the money again. Five thousand pounds doesn't take up much room. She went to the desk she called hers, though everything in this house was really Alex's, found a large brown envelope and put the money inside. The envelope could have held twice the amount. It wasn't so bad when she couldn't see the money. When it was hidden. She took her own clothes out of the case, set some aside for washing, some for dry-cleaning.

The phone rang. She jumped and caught her breath. It would be him. It would be Trevor Lant. What could she say? Very afraid, she picked up the phone, her hand shaking.

Her voice came, breathy and shrill. 'Hello?'

It was her mother. 'I said I'd phone. Give you a chance to get home and unpack. How did the wedding go?'

'It was fine.'

'You don't sound fine. Have you got a cold?'

Polly longed to tell her. She couldn't. She knew what her mother would say: tell Alex, tell the police, say what you've done and make it all right. But first she would say, Polly, how could you? What's wrong with you? 'I'm just tired,' she said, and making an effort, 'How's Dad?'

'Better, I'm glad to say. He thought you might both come over for a meal tonight. Save you cooking.'

Her mother thought she lived like they used to thirty years ago, cooking meat and two veg, making desserts. She would know how to make a fire, burn things . . . 'Can we make it some other night? Tomorrow?'

'Of course, darling.'

'I'll phone.'

When she had put the phone down, the house seemed very quiet. There was no noise from the street, no wind blowing, no footsteps, no traffic sounds. It was as if she had gone deaf.

The silence made her long for sound. She put out one finger and tapped the bedhead. The tiny tap made her jump again. Then she said aloud, 'What shall I do?'

Not what her mother would have told her to do. Not what Alex would have told her. Still, it was plain she couldn't keep the money. Every moment it was in this house she was stealing it. If she took it to a police station and said what she had done, they would think she was mad. They would arrest her. She imagined their faces, staring at her as they asked her to say again what she had said. You took a man's case? But why? What were you thinking of? That was stealing – did you know that? She knew she couldn't go to the police. But she must do something. Find out where Trevor Lant lived? Yes, that was it. Find out where he lived and get his money back to him.

The phone book first. If he wasn't there she would try the Internet. He might not live in London. Still, she would try her own phone book first, the one for West London. Her hand shook as she turned the pages. Lanson, Lanssens, Lant . . . There were four Lants listed, one in Notting Hill, one in Maida Vale, one in

Bayswater and a T.H. Lant nearer to her own house than any of them. Only half a mile or so away, in Willesden. But could she be sure it was him? She could phone and when he answered, say, 'Trevor Lant?'

He would know her voice. She knew she would be much too afraid to phone him. Could she get someone else to do it? Not Alex, not her mother or her father. A friend? Roz? Louise? They would want to know why. The address in the phone book looked like a house, not a flat. Number 34 Bristol Road, NW2. Why had she got this crazy idea that she would know it was his house when she saw it? Did she think he would have painted it orange?

Of course she couldn't go there. He would recognise her. Not if she wore a long dark coat. Not if she tied her head up in a scarf like the Moslem women wore and put on dark glasses. Was she just going there to look? To make sure the Trevor Lant whose money she had, lived there? And how would she do that?

It was only four-thirty in the afternoon but dark by now. She should go soon if she meant to be back when Alex came home. If she was going to return Trevor Lant's money she should also

41

return his clothes. Keeping them was stealing too. Outside it was icy in the bitter wind. Her hands shaking again, she took the plastic bag out of the wastebin and for the first time looked at what was inside. Two T-shirts, two pairs of underpants, two pairs of socks, the yellow shirt he had worn on the flight out and a red shirt. She wrote a note for Alex in case she wasn't home in time: *Gone to Louise's. Back soon.* He had never liked Louise. He wouldn't phone her.

Alex had the car. She could get to Bristol Road by bus and on foot. Suddenly she was aware of how tired she was. Of course she had hardly slept at all last night and she hadn't been able to sleep when she got home. A drink would help. He had called her an alcoholic and maybe he was right. Who cared? When all this was over and the money and the clothes were back with him, she'd give up drinking. Alex would like that. No more gin, though. Not at this hour, as her mother might say. She opened a bottle of red wine and poured herself a big glass.

When she had drunk half the wine she put on her long black coat, wrapped a grey and black scarf round her head and put on dark sunglasses. This get-up made her look strange but round here a great many people looked strange. Should she take the money and the clothes with her? And then what? Leave them on his doorstep? No, find some other way of returning them. She put the envelope in the drawer of her desk, the clothes inside the washing machine, and drank the rest of the wine.

She had to wait a long time for the bus. About twenty people were waiting, mostly in silence, tired people who had been at work all day. It was very cold and a few thin flakes of snow were falling. She was glad of the scarf she had wrapped round her head. A woman stared at her as if she'd never seen dark glasses before but Polly kept them on even when the bus came. Most people inside the bus sat silent, looking gloomy, but some chattered and laughed, drank from fizzy drink bottles, ate crisps, sandwiches, chocolate. Babies cried, children climbed over people and over seats. One of the little girls was the age Polly had been when she cut up the library book. She got off a long way from Bristol Road and began to walk.

A lot of women were dressed like her, without the glasses. No one took any notice of her. Once she had turned down a side street there were no more people. Cars were parked nose to tail all along both sides. Lights shone dimly behind coloured curtains. A long-dead Christmas tree had been thrown out on the pavement with rubbish bags. She had looked up Bristol Road in the street atlas and was sure she knew the way but it seemed a very long way. She kept thinking she would meet him coming along. Or the footsteps following her would be his. She turned round once and then again but no one was there. When she reached the corner and saw the street name, Bristol Road, she felt too afraid to go on. Her watch told her it was nearly six. Alex would be home in ten minutes.

She clenched her icy hands, wishing she had brought gloves. She forced herself to walk, to push one foot in front of the other. Bristol Road seemed darker than the streets she had come along. The street lamps had long spaces between them. There were more trees and in front gardens there were evergreens, the kind you see in graveyards, the kind that never lose their black leaves. The sunglasses she wore made the darkness darker but she was afraid to take them off. It was a long street and she had come into it at number 188. It seemed like miles to 34 but at last she was outside its gate. Or outside the gate of 32, not daring to get too close. She held on to a fence post like an old woman afraid she might fall.

No lights were on in the house. It was in deep darkness and its front garden was full of dark bushes. A little light from a street lamp shone on the windows so that they looked like black glass. Of all the houses on this side only number 34 had a brightly painted front door. It was hard to tell the exact colour but it seemed to be yellow, the yellow of food, an egg yolk or a piece of cheese.

Plainly, no one was at home. She went almost on tip-toe up to the front window and tried to look inside. It was too dark to see much, just the shapes of dull heavy chairs and tables. She looked to see if there was a name under the doorbell but there was nothing. The phone book had said a T.H. Lant lived here, not that *he* did. It might be a Thomas or Tim Lant. She had no way of knowing. He might not even live in London but up north somewhere or in Wales or by the sea. She would have to come back in daylight. Tomorrow was Saturday and she could come then.

What would she say to Alex? Make some excuse. You mean, tell some lie, she said to herself. But she would *have* to. Suppose Alex were in her position, he would have to lie. But he wouldn't be, she told herself as she walked back to the bus stop, feeling weak and tired. He would never do the things I do . . .

CHAPTER FIVE

ON THE WAY HOME she thought, suppose I find the police waiting for me? I can explain, she thought. I can tell them he gave it to me. Or I can say I know nothing about it. And if they want to search the house? I'll say it's my money, I'll say those are Alex's clothes . . . Alex opened the front door to her before she got her key out.

'I phoned Louise,' he said. 'I wanted to pick you up, take you out to dinner.' He looked hurt. 'There was something I was planning to ask you.'

Polly thought, he was going to propose to me. He was going to ask me to marry him. For once, she didn't know what to say. It was too late to go out now and she was so tired she thought she could fall asleep standing up.

'You left me a note saying you'd be there.'

'I know. I meant to go.' She was so used to

him trusting her, believing everything she said, that the look on his face shocked her. But she was a good liar. She had had plenty of practice. Coming up close to him, she looked him straight in the eye. 'I got on the bus, the one that goes to Louise's road. It's only two stops. But I was so tired I fell asleep and when I woke up I was in Finchley.'

He believed her. His face had cleared and he laughed, but gently. 'You should have waited for me and I'd have taken you in the car.'

'I know you would.' She had to find out. 'What were you planning to ask me?'

He smiled. 'Don't worry about it. Another time.'

'I really need a drink.'

As she said it she thought of Trevor Lant saying she drank too much. Why had she ever spoken to him? Why hadn't she just kept silent when he spoke to her? Alex brought her a glass of wine.

'Have you eaten?' he asked.

'I don't want anything. I just want to go to bed.'

Suppose he had looked inside the washing machine? Before she went to bed, while Alex

48

was watching the news on TV, she took out Trevor Lant's clothes. She put them in a bag and put the bag in the bottom of her wardrobe. Tired as she was, she couldn't sleep. How to get away on her own for an hour or two in the morning? Just to go back to Bristol Road, see it in daylight, maybe talk to someone next door and find out who lived there. Alex slept beside her, still and silent as he always was. He wants to marry me, she thought. We've never really talked about it but I know he does. He'll ask me sometime this weekend. I shall say yes. Of course I will. And when we're engaged I'll make a vow to tell no more lies and never, ever steal anything again. The wine I drink at my wedding will be the last I'll ever drink.

She slept badly, and woke up to find him gone. She thought, I could tell him. I could tell him now. But no, she couldn't. Tell him she had stolen a man's case? Taken money and clothes out of it, brought them here, hidden them and gone to find where he lived? And it's not the first time, she would have to say. I took my aunt's book. I took a man's Walkman and threw it under a truck. I took Abby Robinson's watch and smashed it and gave myself this scar.

And I took other things, I took them to get back at people, a handbag from Louise once because she didn't ask me to her party. I threw it over the bridge into the canal. Alex would tell me I'm mad. Perhaps I *am* mad. He wouldn't want to be married to a woman like me.

Alex came in with tea for her. He was smiling. 'Had a good night?'

'I'm fine,' she said.

He seemed to have forgotten her note and the things she had said. 'I thought we could go out this morning and buy those books I need.'

I once stole a book and cut the pages to pieces because my aunt smacked me. Look at my finger. That's the scar where I cut myself . . . What would he do if she said that?

'You go,' she said. 'You won't need me.'

No bus this morning. He had taken the tube and left the car behind. She could say she had taken it to go shopping. On the way back from Bristol Road she could *go* shopping, make her lies true. She felt safer inside the car. Turning the corner into Lant's street she saw his car on the driveway before she saw the house, it was such a bright colour. A bright peacock blue, the kind of blue that hurts your eyes. And the front door, in daylight, was a sharper yellow than egg yolk.

So it *was* his house. It seemed to be. He liked bright colours, orange cases, yellow door, peacock blue car. Because she was in the car she wasn't wearing the scarf, the long coat and the sunglasses. She drove round again, slowly this time, on his side of the road. And saw just inside the rear window of his car his small carry-on case. His orange carry-on case.

That told her all she needed to know. He lived there. It was his house. All she had to do now was get it all back to him, the clothes – she would wash and iron his clothes – and the money. Driving away from Bristol Road, she thought of sending it by post. The post had been bad lately. Suppose the money got lost in the post? Find another way then, of getting it back. Someone at the wheel of a passing car hooted at her. What had she done? She didn't know. Anyway, it wasn't him, it wasn't Lant. The driver who had hooted was in a black car. She drove into the Tesco car park and went in, pushing her trolley between the fruit and vegetable racks.

If only I can get the money back to him, she

thought, and not be seen, I will never take anything again. No, not 'take' – 'steal'. Use the proper word, she told herself. I stole that money just as I stole Tom's Walkman and Louise's bag. But this has cured me. I will never do it again. It was funny how when you saw something unusual like his car, you soon saw others like it. She'd never before seen a car quite the colour of his but there was one in the Tesco car park, bright peacock blue.

Driving home, she tried to think of ways to get the money back. If his car was there, he was in. If it wasn't, he was out. That might not always be so. The car might be away being serviced or lent to a friend or in a lock-up garage somewhere. She would have to watch the house until she saw him go out. Put the money into small envelopes and once he was gone, put the envelopes through the letterbox in that yellow front door. And his clothes, neatly ironed, the yellow shirt and the red one and the orange T-shirt.

Why hadn't he told the police? That puzzled her. He must guess it was Polly who had taken his case. She had been flying club class so he would know she had got off the aircraft before

52

him. When his case couldn't be found the first person he would think of would be her. And then when they found his case in the ladies' . . . They would tell him that, and he would go straight to the airport police. So why hadn't they phoned or come here? Perhaps they had. Another peacock blue car was behind her, two cars behind her, and for a moment she felt afraid. But once she was home it had gone.

The look on Alex's face when she went in scared her. He was hardly ever angry but he looked angry now. She thought, he has been to my desk and found the money. Or the police have been here. But she was wrong. It was only that his computer had crashed and he had to call for help. Smiling now, pleased to see her, he helped her in with the bags of shopping.

'You didn't tell me we're going to see your parents tonight.'

She had forgotten. 'I forgot,' she said. 'Don't you want to? I can put them off.'

'No, I'd like to go. It's just that we said we'd go and see that film. I suppose we could go first. Shall we?'

She must keep watch on Lant's house. She had meant to go back this afternoon, see if his car was gone or stay there until he came out and drove away. Then she could put the money through his letter box . . . It would have to wait, that was all. Wait all through Sunday? She wasn't due at work until midday on Monday but must she wait until Monday morning?

'Did you get a paper?'

'I forgot,' she said again. 'I'll go out again.'

'No, I'll go.'

Never before had she been so glad to see him go out. To leave her on her own. Always, in the past, she had wanted him with her. She had felt lonely and lost without him. Now his going out was a relief. She ran to her desk and opened the drawer where the money was.

She called it 'her' desk because she used it but in fact it was Alex's. Almost everything in the house was Alex's, the carpets, the curtains, the tables and chairs and beds and the kitchen things. It was just as it had been when she moved in with him. She had brought only a radio with her, a lamp or two, and some china and glass. The desk she had taken over because she was the one who sometimes worked from home. As far as she knew, he never went near it.

And he had not been near it that morning.

The money was just as she had left it. Why had Lant wanted it in pounds, dollars and euros? It didn't matter. She found some envelopes, ten of them, and put the money into them, five hundred pounds in each one. Alex might never go near the desk but still the money wasn't safe there. She took the ten envelopes upstairs and put them in her underwear drawer. Then she checked on Lant's clothes. They were where she had left them, at the back of her wardrobe. If she did the washing now, his with hers, Alex might see Lant's yellow shirt and the orange T-shirt when she took them out of the machine. Better wait till tomorrow . . .

He was back with his paper just as she was coming downstairs. As they walked together into the living room the phone rang. Again she thought, it will be the police. Or Lant himself. Lant. He knows. He must have seen me this morning. She picked up the phone and said, 'Hello?'

Alex was standing behind her. She said into the phone, 'Who is that?' There was silence, no heavy breathing, just silence. 'Who *is* it?' Her voice sounded strained, panicky. There was no answer and she put the phone down.

She turned to Alex. He had sat down, the paper on his knees.

'Who was that?' he said. 'Was it someone you knew?'

'I don't know who it was,' she said, her eyes meeting his. 'He didn't speak.'

'He?'

'He, she, I told you I don't know. They didn't say anything.'

That had been a mistake, a bad mistake for a good liar to make.

Alex said in his quiet gentle way, 'When my friend George was married to his first wife, they got a lot of phone calls from one of these silent callers. If he answered, there was no one there. When she answered while George was with her she would say 'Who is that?' but got no answer either. Of course he didn't know what she said when he *wasn't* with her.'

'I don't understand,' Polly said, though she did.

'Oh, well,' said Alex. 'Soon after that she went off with a chap she'd been seeing.'

After they had had lunch they went to the cinema.

Polly watched the film but after it was over

she couldn't have said what it was about or even who was in it. She was thinking about the money and Lant's clothes and the phone call. Above all, the phone call. She had never had a phone call like it before. It must have been Lant. He hadn't said a word, but she knew it was Lant. He might not have seen her that morning, but he had guessed it was she who had taken his case. Somehow he had found out where she lived. Not from the phone book. Only Alex's name was in the phone book. This address was on her bags while she was waiting in the check-in queues. He must have noted it down either going to New York or coming back. But no, that must have been him in the car park. That must have been him following her. So he would know her address. Why? Because he too would want revenge?

Her address but not her phone number . . . Directory Enquiries would have given him that. Dial one-one-eight, five hundred. Get the voters' list online, then give Alex's name and address. It was easy. What would Lant do next?

Why hadn't he been to the police? What was he doing? Maybe it was something to do with the money. It might not be his. He might have stolen it. If that was the case, the last people he would go to were the police. That must be the answer.

She felt a huge relief. Lant wouldn't tell the police because the money wasn't his. But she must get it back to him. Polly thought of all the films she had seen in which gangsters had money stolen from them. Money they had stolen, but which they still thought of as theirs. The first thing they did was get revenge. Lant would do what her father called taking the law into his own hands . . .

She must get the money back to him. But she must do it soon. She dared not wait till Monday. That would give him all tomorrow to get his revenge.

She must do it now. Lant might come here and harm her or, worse, Alex. As they came out of the cinema Alex said, 'I didn't think much of that, did you? Not the way that woman acted. Real life isn't like that.'

'No,' she said. 'No, you're right.'

She could remember very little of it but she knew real life wasn't like that.

CHAPTER SIX

'I HAVE TO GO out again,' she said.

Alex said, 'OK, I'll come with you.'

'Oh, no, I'm going to Louise's. You won't want to come. You don't like her. I borrowed a pashmina from her before I went away and I ought to take it back.'

He said, his face a blank, 'I promise not to phone her this time.'

Polly didn't know what to say. She smiled, her face stiff, remembering. It had been Louise's birthday, her twenty-fifth. Polly had sent her a birthday card but knew nothing about the party. It was Roz who had gone to the party and, thinking Polly couldn't go, had told her about it next day. Polly remembered how hurt she had been and how angry. Not to be asked, and she was Louise's best friend! Next time she was at Louise's she went into her bedroom and took the handbag. On the way home – it was before she knew Alex – she stopped on the canal bridge in the dark. Holding the bag over the side, she let it slip down into the black shiny water. She could still hear the sound of the splash and feel a drop of water from the spray. Later she found out Louise had sent her a card, inviting her, but it had got lost in the post.

'We're due at your parents at seven.' Alex kissed her. 'Don't be long.'

'I won't,' she said. His kiss seemed to burn her as if she was guilty of some crime against him.

She was. She had lied to him again. She ran upstairs, took the money out of her underwear drawer and put it into the biggest bag she had. It was only when she was outside and in the car that she realised she had forgotten Lant's clothes. They were still dirty. She would wash them tomorrow and send them back to him by post. How easy all this would be if she – and Lant – had come back from New York on a Wednesday, if today was Thursday and Alex was at work. As it was, nothing was easy. She mustn't be long. She mustn't give Alex reason to suspect her again.

Lant's bright blue car was still on his driveway, just as it had been in the morning, but the orange carry-on bag was no longer inside it. It was later now than she had been yesterday, very cold but dry and the sky clear. Far above the street lamps and the bare tree branches she could see the curve of a bright white moon. Lights were on upstairs and down in Lant's house. Behind the curtains those lights looked orange, the colour he loved. She sat in the dark car on the other side of the street and a little way up. A car was parked in front of hers and one behind hers. If he looked out of that orange window he wouldn't be able to see her.

As the engine cooled the inside of the car grew cold. She began to shake with cold, wishing she had worn a warmer coat. It was just a quarter past six. She had hoped his car would be gone, his house in darkness, and she would quickly have been able to return the money. Suppose she were to drive round a bit, just to have the heater on. She would get warm but he might go out while she was away. It would be better to *see* him go out. She shivered with the cold, rubbed her hands, and her upper arms.

At twenty to seven the upstairs light in his house went out. The two downstairs lights stayed on, the one in the front room and the one she could see in his hallway, through the glass panel above the front door. She drew a deep breath, sick with waiting. Her hands were cold as ice. It seemed like hours before that front room light went out. In fact it was ten minutes. She thought, he must go now, please let him go now, or I shall be late and then what shall I say to Alex?

I could phone him. I could phone my mother. And say what? That I'm stuck in a traffic jam? I can't leave here now, not when he'll come out at any minute. His hallway light stayed on. Maybe he left it on when he went out. People did that, *she* did that, to make burglars think someone was at home. The only thief here was herself . . .

The front door opened and he came out. She thought, now I know for sure it's him. I wasn't quite sure before but now I know. In the light from a street lamp and the glass panel above his front door, she saw he was wearing the same black suit with a camel coat over it. His shirt was red, his tie red and black. He didn't look her way but got into his car, started the engine and turned on the headlights. It was three minutes to seven when he drove away.

62

She didn't waste any time but got out of her car, walked quickly across the street and up to the front door. On the doorstep she thought, maybe someone is in and they'll come to the door when I open the letter box. Trying to be very quiet, she pushed open the flap and put the first envelope in. No one came. There was silence. The other envelopes next, one, two, three. She thought she heard a sound from inside and her hand shook again, the way it had from the cold. Maybe there was no one there. He could have a dog or a cat that made that noise. She waited, listened. Nothing. She put the rest of the envelopes through, heard the last of them fall on to the mat.

It was five past seven.

Almost at once she moved into that build-up of traffic she meant to tell Alex about. But she was late already. Every traffic light turned red as she came up to it. The line of cars went very slowly. A light that was red for the first car had turned red again by the time she got there. In horror she watched the hand of the clock move from twenty past to twenty-five past. Lurching and jumping over the speed bumps, she reached home at twenty-five to eight. The front door was open. Alex was waiting for her on the step.

He said nothing, only shook his head a little. She ran upstairs, changed into a long skirt and sweater, combed her hair, and was in the car with him three minutes later.

'I phoned your mother,' he said, his voice cold. 'I said we'd be late. I didn't know how late.'

'I can explain,' she said. 'The traffic was terrible. I was as quick as I could be.'

He didn't reply. She thought, I wonder if he phoned Louise. I can't ask. I can never ask. The worst is over, anyway. I've given Lant back his money. Tomorrow I'll wash his clothes and iron them and on Monday morning I'll send them back. I'll never go near Bristol Road again. I'll never steal anything again or lie again or drink again, not when all this is over.

As he drove Alex said, 'Someone phoned. A man. It was about half an hour after you went out. He said he was the Komodo dragon and then he put the phone down.'

She thought she would scream and put her hand over her mouth to stop herself. Alex had his eyes on the road. 'I don't much care for jokes like that,' he said. 'The Komodo dragon is great, a wonderful big lizard, not something to make you laugh or shudder.'

Polly's voice came out like a squeak. 'I don't know who it was,' she lied.

'Maybe it was a wrong number. We seem to get a lot of those lately, don't we?'

He didn't speak another word all the way to her parents' house. He frowned when her father handed her a big glass of wine almost as soon as they were inside. She thought of Lant calling her an alcoholic. Did it mean you were an alcoholic if you needed a drink as much as she did? I did drink a lot on that flight, she thought. Alex hardly drinks at all. If we're always going to be together – and we are, please, we always are – I must drink less. I'll keep to what I said and drink my last glass at my wedding.

But she gulped down the wine. That was the second time Lant had phoned but, if Alex was right, the call had been made before she gave the money back. He would leave her alone now he had his money. He'd forget her, put all this behind him.

Her mother had made a big meal for them.

Leek and potato soup first, then roast lamb, then a lemon tart. Before she took the money back Polly wouldn't have been able to eat. She could now, in spite of that second phone call. Lant had only called because he wanted his money. She was hungry and her father was refilling her wineglass to the brim.

Alex was talking now about the film they'd seen, telling her parents they ought to see it. Polly could remember nothing about it. She might as well not have been there. Then her father said something which made her blush and stare.

'You seem to have had a busy day, Polly. I saw you in Willesden this morning. I hooted and waved but you were lost in a dream.'

Deny it? A man doesn't mistake someone else for his own daughter.

'I didn't see you, Dad,' she said, not daring to look at Alex.

She remembered the black car which had hooted at her. She had thought it was her bad driving. Finishing the wine in her glass she thought, I would like to drink myself drunk, to sleep, not to have to drive home with Alex.

But she had to. As they moved out on to the

66

road, he said, 'We have to talk, Polly.'

'Do we?'

'When we get home.'

I've never loved him so much as I do now, she thought, already in a panic. I love him. I can't lose him. He was going to ask me to marry him. Will he ask me now?

At home he said to her, in a voice she had never heard before, a voice that was cold and distant, 'I suppose you'll want another drink?'

'No,' she said. 'I've had too much.'

'At least you know it and that's something. Sit down then.' He sat facing her and took both her hands in his. 'A lot of strange things have been going on. Let's talk about it.'

Feeling her hands held in his made her feel better at once. 'Talk about what?'

'Well, I believed your story about falling asleep on the bus. But I don't believe it now. You said you were shopping this morning, but your dad saw you in Willesden. And this evening. You didn't go to Louise's. Louise told me on Friday she was away for the weekend. She was just leaving when I phoned. And then there was that fool who said he was the Komodo dragon. What's going on, Polly?'

'Nothing's going on. Really and truly. It's nothing.'

He kept hold of her hands. 'Are you seeing someone else?'

'Oh, no, of course not. Of course I'm not.'

'Sure? I'd rather know now.'

'There's nothing to know. I *promise* you. I love you, Alex. There couldn't be anyone else, not ever.'

'It's just that when you went to New York to Lizzie's wedding I thought, I could go too but she won't want me. If she'd wanted me, why didn't she ask? Is she meeting some man in New York? Is he coming back with her? And then when I met you at Heathrow you were so pleased to see me, you looked so happy, I thought I must be wrong.'

'You were wrong,' she said. 'You'd been so generous, buying me a ticket in club class. I was so grateful that I didn't want to go and leave you.' She clutched at his hands, lifted them to her lips and kissed them. 'I've never known you jealous before.'

'Oh, I was. I always was. I didn't let you see, that's all.'

CHAPTER SEVEN

LIGHT-HEARTED NOW, SHE got up early, had the washing in the machine by eight, her washing and Alex's and Lant's clothes. It's going to be a good day, she thought. The sun was shining and it was less cold. There were pink flowers on the tree in the garden next door and tulips coming out in tubs. She took a cup of tea up to Alex. He would stay in bed to drink it while she took the things out of the washing machine. Just in case he noticed Lant's clothes.

They shared the housework. He might say he would do the ironing. So she quickly ironed Lant's yellow shirt and a green one. By the time Alex came down, Lant's clothes were packed in a plastic bag and wrapped in brown paper, ready for the post.

It was like spring outside. She walked about, touching the new buds on the trees, smelling the air. Now everything was cleared up, she thought, Alex would ask her to marry him. He would probably ask her today. When she had taken up his tea he had said something about taking her out to lunch. It was to be at a pub on the river. Or he might wait until this evening to ask her. After dark was more romantic. They could have a June wedding. Where would they go on honeymoon? Not New York, definitely not New York, though it was said to be nice in June.

She went inside and found Alex in the kitchen.

'You've been busy,' he said. 'Do you want me to iron that lot?'

'If you like.'

It felt so good having nothing else to be afraid of, to know that she could tell the truth now. I will never tell any more lies, she said to herself. I will never tell him I've been somewhere I haven't been or done something I haven't done. I will change. I will be a different person. I will be the person he thought I was before last Friday.

He had started on the ironing, had already ironed a shirt of his own. Now he pulled out from the basket an orange T-shirt. It was Lant's.

She had missed it when she was ironing his clothes. She had done all the rest and packed them but she had missed this T-shirt. Alex lifted it up, looked at it.

'Is this yours, Polly?'

'Yes, of course,' she lied.

'A strange colour for you. Did you buy it in New York?'

'Yes, I did.'

'It looks a bit big for you. Is that the fashion?'

She nodded, sick of verbal lying.

'D'you know what that colour reminds me of?' Alex laid the T-shirt down on the ironing board. 'It reminds me of that man we saw at Heathrow. Do you remember? At the check-in? He was wearing a black suit and he had an orange case. Do you remember?'

She knew her face had gone red. 'Maybe,' she said. 'I think I do.'

'You said it'd be easy to find. You couldn't miss it.'

'Did I?'

She wished he hadn't said that. It cast a cloud over the day. While they were talking the sun had gone in. The sky was grey now. It looked like rain. Alex was ironing the T-shirt,

71

taking special care with it because it was hers. He was better at ironing than she was. When he had finished he fetched a hanger from the hallway cupboard and hung the T-shirt on it.

'There,' he said. 'Now you can wear it when we go out.'

She tried to smile. 'Oh, no, it's not warm enough. It's for summer.'

Upstairs she folded it and put it inside the parcel she would send to Lant. Now, for the first time, she began to think of him as a human being. A person with feelings, needs, loves, pain. It must have been a huge shock to him when he got his orange case back without the money. When he knew he'd lost all that money. What had he done about it? Anything? Had he told the police? He must have. Polly hadn't thought about the police since that first time, when she had come home on Friday evening and had thought they might be waiting for her. Maybe they were looking for her now . . .

But she had given the money back. Every pound and dollar and euro of it. And tomorrow she was going to send him his clothes back.

Washed and ironed and neatly folded. Really, she had done him a favour. No harm had been done. All the harm had been to her and she remembered the stream of hot coffee he had poured on her cream trousers. Forget his feelings, his needs, she told herself. Forget his loves and pain. It's all over.

And she was better. Thanks to being with Alex, she was doing better. She hadn't acted as she had over Auntie Pauline's library book, cutting it into pieces. She hadn't cut Lant's money to pieces. Or destroyed it as she had Tom's Walkman and Abby's watch. She hadn't dropped it over the canal bridge as she had Louise's bag. She had taken his money back and would send the clothes back. It would have been easier to destroy the money and the clothes but she hadn't. If she could have told Alex everything, all of it from Auntie Pauline's book to Lant's money, he would have seen how much better she was now than she used to be. He would also think she had lost her mind. She could never tell him.

She dressed carefully for going out in a pale blue suit. Why did men always like you in blue? She didn't know. But she was sure that when she went downstairs Alex would say, 'You look lovely.'

It was strange how strong the urge to explain to him was. Only by telling him everything could she protect herself and be truly safe. Then if the police came he would know why. He and she would be in it together. I love that word, she thought, that word 'together'. One day, when Alex and I have been together for years, then I will tell him. When we are old I will tell him. And if he finds out long before that? I must take that risk, she thought. Isn't life one risk after another?

She went downstairs. Alex, who had finished the ironing and was sitting at the table reading the paper, said, 'You look lovely.'

'Shall we go, then?'

'I want to stop off on the way home and buy things for dinner tonight. We're going to have a special dinner.'

He was very romantic. He would probably go down on one knee. She remembered something. Two days before she went to America she had mislaid one of her rings. It had turned up next day and she had no idea why she couldn't find it before. Now she understood. Alex had 'borrowed' it to buy an engagement ring the same size.

On the way back from lunch it started to rain. A fine drizzle at first, then a downpour. Polly stayed in the car while Alex went into shops buying smoked salmon, a duck, salad and fruit. He bought champagne too and a bottle of dessert wine. He would drink very little. It was mostly for her.

She thought about sending Lant's clothes back next day. Register the package perhaps? He would go to work, surely. She could take them back just as she had taken the money. Alex began the drive home. The traffic, usually light on a Sunday, was heavy because it was raining.

'Why do you always get traffic jams when it's wet?'

'I don't know,' he said. 'No one knows. It's one of the mysteries of life.'

If she had taken Auntie Pauline's book back and told her what she'd done, her life wouldn't have changed. Everything would have been much the same. If she'd told Abby Robinson that she was the one who had stolen her watch and had offered to pay for it, what would Abby have done? Nothing much, probably. Screamed and hit her perhaps. But Abby would have calmed down and taken the money. On the other hand, if she'd not taken Tom's Walkman and thrown it under a truck, life might have been utterly changed. They'd have stayed together. They might have married. She'd never have met Alex. So did that mean what she did was sometimes a good thing? Lying and stealing had brought her to Alex . . .

They were turning the corner into their street now. He had lived in this house for four years before they met. He had laid the carpets and bought the furniture as if he was making it ready for her. It would be her home for years now. Perhaps they would live there always, bring up their children there. Alex turned in at the gate and she looked up. Parked outside the house was a car the same colour as Lant's, the same bright peacock blue. You didn't see that shade very often.

She looked again. What she saw made her feel sick. It *was* Lant's car and Lant was sitting in the driving seat.

CHAPTER EIGHT

ALEX GOT OUT, TOOK the shopping out of the boot, came round and opened the door on the passenger side for her. He always did that. She had to get out, though she would have liked the earth to open and close over her head. Alex said, 'Let's get inside before it starts raining again.'

She followed him, not looking behind her. He unlocked the front door. A hand on her shoulder made her spin round. Trevor Lant stood there on the path. Today he was wearing a bright red jacket. He looked her straight in the eye, the way she looked at people when she lied, but he didn't speak to her. He said to Alex, 'Who the hell are you?'

'What did you say?'

'I asked who the hell you are.'

'I might ask you the same question. This is my house.'

'And the woman with you is my girlfriend.' Again Lant put a hand on her shoulder. 'Thanks for bringing the money back, darling. That's all I came for. You've still got some of my clothes but you can bring them back when you come over tonight.'

Polly tried to speak but she couldn't. She was shaking all over. She knew she had changed colour, but she couldn't tell if she had gone red or white. Lant said, 'Who is this chap, anyway? Your ex, I suppose.'

'Go,' Alex said in a voice she had never heard before. 'Go or I'll call the police.'

Lant shrugged. 'I'd say I don't admire your taste in men, Polly, only you've got me now.' He turned away, laughing. 'You've got your dragon now. I'll see you later.'

As the rain began again, he went back down the path, let himself out of the gate and got into his car. Everything in the street was grey but for his red jacket and his bright blue car. Alex went into the house and she stumbled in after him.

Her voice, which had gone and left her dumb, came back, a poor little thin voice. 'I can explain.'

'What is there to explain?' He sounded very tired.

He went into the kitchen and began taking all the things he had bought out of the bags and putting them in the fridge. Her voice gaining strength, she said, 'I really can explain, Alex. It's not what you think.'

He left what he was doing and looked at her. It was a stranger's face, one she thought she had never seen before.

'Let me tell you what I think,' he said. 'I know who that man was. I recognised him, though I don't know his name. He was the man at Heathrow with the orange bag. I think you met on the flight. Or maybe you knew each other before and arranged to meet at the airport. Anyway, you spent your time in New York with him. You saw him on Friday night, on Saturday morning and last night. I don't know where the money comes into this or the clothes but it doesn't matter. You can go off with him now. You won't have to tell me any more lies.'

'Alex, it wasn't like that. I took his bag at Heathrow. On the way back. And I had to get it back to him . . .'

Her voice failed and grew hoarse. Of course

he wouldn't believe her. No one would believe her. She would have to tell him the whole thing, from the start of it when she was eight.

'My aunt hit me in the garden, so I stole her book and cut up the pages and . . .'

'Spare me this, Polly,' he said. 'I don't know where your aunt comes into this or your stealing that man's bag. It's all lies, isn't it? I know you tell lies. I've always known it but I thought you'd begun to change. I was wrong, that's all.'

'Alex, don't. Don't talk like this. That man is nothing to me. I barely know him. It's true I went to New York with him and came back with him. I've been to his house too but it's not the way you think . . .'

'Was that his T-shirt I ironed?'

'Yes, it was but I can explain . . .'

He didn't wait to hear what she had to say. She heard him talking to someone on the phone in the next room but not what he was saying. Then he went upstairs. Somehow she had to make him see. If she were to phone Lant, tell him about her and Alex, how she loved Alex, tell him they were going to be married, surely then . . . But that wouldn't work. Lant had come here on purpose to make Alex think he and Polly were having an affair. That was *his* revenge. He had seen, and now she could see, that everything she had done after stealing his case, made it look as if they were lovers. Her trips to his house, the lies she told, his clothes that she still had, the truth she had to tell, that he and she had gone to New York together and come back on the same flight. Could he somehow have followed her when she put the money through his door and had seen Alex waiting for her on the step?

Upstairs, Alex was in their bedroom, putting things into a case. She thought of how many times she had seen this scene in a film. The person who was leaving packing a case. The one who was left watching him do it. She felt cold in the warm room and as sick as she had when she first opened Lant's case.

'I'm going to my sister's,' Alex said. 'I just phoned her.'

'Alex, are you saying you're leaving me?'

'You've left me, haven't you?'

'Of course I haven't. I told you, this is all a stupid mistake.'

'You haven't had money from this man? You

81

haven't got some of his clothes? You don't know where he lives?'

'Yes to all that, but I can explain . . .'

'I know,' he said, 'that what you're going to say will be a lie. So don't say it. At least don't make a fool of yourself now. Not when we're parting.' He closed the case.

Polly took hold of him by the arm. She held on to him with both hands as if she could keep him with her by force. 'Don't say that, please don't. I can explain if you'll let me.'

'Let me go, Polly. We're better apart. We've been happy in this house but I don't want to live here any more. You'll be with him wherever it is he lives. I shall probably sell this place, but it's too early to say . . .'

She was crying. She hung on to him and tried to stop him going. Gently, he pulled himself away, prised her hands off him. She fell on the bed and sobbed. Alex went down the stairs and she heard the front door close.

CHAPTER NINE

How could he do this to me? she asked herself as she lay there. How could he? I explained. I explained as much as he'd let me. He wouldn't listen. At any rate, Trevor Lant had a reason for doing what he did. He wanted revenge on me because I took his money. Giving it back wasn't enough for him. He wanted revenge and I can understand that. I know all about revenge. But Alex . . .

He had been totally unreasonable. She had told him she could explain and she had tried to but he wouldn't listen. He had believed Lant but not her. Just because she sometimes told lies. Everyone told lies – except him. She hadn't asked him to have such high standards for her. Who was he to judge her? Who was he to break up her whole world in ten minutes?

That morning he had been going to ask her to marry him. He would have bought the ring. She got up from the bed and looked out of the window. He had taken the car. It was his car, but how did he think she was to get around? It was cruel what he had done and she hated him for it.

An idea came to her and she moved across to 'his' chest of drawers. Well, all the furniture was his, but this was the chest he kept his own things in. She opened one drawer after another. His clothes were in them, socks, ties, sweaters, all but the bottom drawer which he had emptied when he packed. She tried the bedside cabinet on his side. A book, an old wallet, a watch he never wore. He hadn't taken any of his suits and only one jacket. She went through the pockets of his raincoat, his leather jacket. All the pockets were empty except for one in his overcoat. There was a jeweller's box in there, a little square box of red velvet.

She lifted its lid. The ring was inside. It was made of gold with a single large square-cut diamond. He knew her size so it would fit. It did and she slipped it on. The light caught the diamond and made a rainbow on the wall. She would never have the right to wear it now. He would come back for the rest of his clothes when he knew she'd be at work, take the ring away and give it to some other woman. Wherever he went to live he would need his furniture, so he would take that too. All the love she had had for him turned to hate.

She would have liked to have a big van come round. The men in it would take out all his tables and chairs and glass and china and put it in the van. They would take it somewhere, it didn't matter where, and she would smash it all up. There was no van and no men. She was on her own but she could still do it.

She went downstairs and into the living room. With one movement of her arm, she swept all the ornaments off a shelf. Glass broke and china and the leg came off a wooden horse. He had broken up her world and she would break up his. It would be the biggest destruction she had ever done. She picked up the CD player and hurled it against the wall, pulled the CDs out of their sleeves and bent them in two. The TV screen was tough but it broke the second time she kicked it. The glass in the pictures cracked when she stamped on them. She pulled his books from the shelves and tore off their covers.

At first it seemed there wasn't much she could do to his furniture, but she fetched a sharp carving knife from the kitchen and slashed at the chair covers, scored grooves in the wood, stabbed at cushions and let their stuffing out. The curtains hung in ribbons when she had used the kitchen scissors on them. After that she ran about the house, the knife in her hand, slashing at everything she came upon. She pulled open the drawer of the drinks cabinet, poured vodka down her throat, smashed the necks of red wine bottles against the fridge and the oven, poured the wine over the pale carpet.

She drank from the broken bottles too, cutting her mouth. The drink got to her at last, making her wild at first, then stupid, dizzy, flat on the floor among the mess. She lay there, unconscious, her arms stretched out and the diamond on her finger winking in the dying light.

WORLD BOOK DAY

Quick Reads

We would like to thank all our partners on the *Quick* Reads project for all their help and support:

BBC RaW
Department for Education and Skills
Trades Union Congress
The Vital Link
The Reading Agency
National Literacy Trust

Quick Reads would also like to thank the Arts Council England and National Book Tokens for their sponsorship.

We would also like to thank the following companies for providing their services free of charge: SX Composing for typesetting all the titles; Icon Reproduction for text reproduction; Norske Skog, Stora Enso, PMS and Iggusend for paper/board supplies; Mackays of Chatham, Cox and Wyman, Bookmarque, White Quill Press, Concise, Norhaven and GGP for the printing.

www.worldbookday.com

Quick Reads

BOOKS IN THE *Quick* Reads SERIES

The Book Boy	Joanna Trollope
Blackwater	Conn Iggulden
Chickenfeed	Minette Walters
Don't Make Me Laugh	Patrick Augustus
Hell Island	Matthew Reilly
How to Change Your Life in 7 Steps	John Bird
Screw It, Let's Do It	Richard Branson
Someone Like Me	Tom Holt
Star Sullivan	Maeve Binchy
The Team	Mick Dennis
The Thief	Ruth Rendell
Woman Walks into a Bar	Rowan Coleman

AND IN MAY 2006

Cleanskin	Val McDermid
Danny Wallace and the Centre of the Universe	Danny Wallace
Desert Claw	Damien Lewis
The Dying Wish	Courttia Newland
The Grey Man	Andy McNab
I Am a Dalek	Gareth Roberts
I Love Football	Hunter Davies
The Name You Once Gave Me	Mike Phillips
The Poison in the Blood	Tom Holland
Winner Takes All	John Francome

Look out for more titles in the *Quick* Reads series in 2007.

www.worldbookday.com

Have you enjoyed reading this
Quick Reads **book?**

Would you like to read more?

Or learn how to write fantastically?

If so, you might like to attend a course to
develop your skills.

Courses are **free** and available in your local area.

If you'd like to find out more,
phone **0800 100 900**.

You can also ask for a **free video or DVD** showing
other people who have been on our courses and
the changes they have made in their lives.

Don't get by – get on.

FIRST CHOICE BOOKS

If you enjoyed this book, you'll find more great reads on www.firstchoicebooks.org.uk. First Choice Books allows you to search by type of book, author and title. So, whether you're looking for romance, sport, humour – or whatever turns you on – you'll be able to find other books you'll enjoy.

You can also borrow books from your local library. If you tell them what you've enjoyed, they can recommend other good reads they think you will like.

First Choice is part of The Vital Link, promoting reading for pleasure. To find out more about The Vital Link visit www.vitallink.org.uk

RaW

Find out what the BBC's RaW (Reading and Writing) campaign has to offer at www.bbc.co.uk/raw

NEW ISLAND

New Island publishers have produced four series of books in its Open Door series – brilliant short novels for adults from the cream of Irish writers. Visit www.newisland.ie and go to the Open Door section.

SANDSTONE PRESS

In the Sandstone Vista Series, Sandstone Press Ltd publish quality contemporary fiction and non-fiction books. The full list can be found at their website www.sandstonepress.com.

Quick Reads

Woman Walks into a Bar
by Rowan Coleman

Arrow

Sometimes the truth is right in front of you.

28-year-old single mother Sam spends her days working in the local supermarket and her Friday nights out with her friends, Joy and Marie, letting her hair down at the White Horse. Life has never been easy for Sam, but she's always hoped that one day she'll meet The One.

After a series of terrible dates with men she's met through an Internet dating agency she's starting to lose heart – until her friends tell her they've set her up on a blind date. Sam's horrified but finally she agrees to go – after all you never know when you might meet the man of your dreams . . .

Quick Reads

How to Change Your Life in 7 Steps
by John Bird

Vermilion

Want to improve your life but don't know where to start? Then this is the book for you.

John Bird explains his seven simple rules that could change your life. You might want to get a new job, stop smoking or go back to college. This book tells you how you can take what you've been given and turn it into something you'll be proud of.